Enid Blyton

BRER RABBIT'S TREASURE
and other stories

This book belongs to

Enid Blyton

BRER RABBIT'S TREASURE

and other stories

Illustrated by Teresa O'Brien

Purnell

Editor: Luigi Bonomi
Designer: Sonja Ferrier
Production: Garry Lewis

A Purnell Book
Text Copyright © 1950 Darrell Waters Ltd
Illustrations Copyright © 1987 Macdonald & Co (Publishers) Ltd
First published in this edition 1987 by
Macdonald & Co (Publishers) Ltd
Greater London House
Hampstead Road
London NW1 7QX
A BPCC plc company

ISBN 0 361 08000X
ISBN 0 361 08000 X Pbk

Printed in Great Britain by
Purnell Book Production Ltd
Member of the BPCC Group

British Library Cataloguing in Publication Data

Blyton, Enid
    Brer Rabbit's treasure and other stories.
    —(Brer Rabbit storybooks)
    I. Title   II. Series
    823'.912[J]   PZ7

Contents: **Page:**

Brer Rabbit's Treasure

ONCE upon a time it got about that Brer Rabbit had a sack of treasure. "He keeps it in his shed," said Brer Fox to Brer Wolf. "I've peeked in the window and, sure enough, there's a sack full of something locked up in there."

"We'll go along each night and see if he has forgotten to lock the shed," said Brer Wolf. "It's certain that he didn't come by that treasure in any right way. We might just as well have it as old Brer Rabbit."

So each night, when it was dark, the pair of them went marching round to Brer Rabbit's shed. But each night the door was locked, and the pair of them didn't like to try and force the door in case Brer Rabbit heard them.

Old Brer Terrapin, who often liked to sleep in a hole near the shed, woke up each night when he heard Brer Fox and Brer Wolf creeping along. He poked out his skinny neck from under his shell, and listened to the pair whispering together.

"Oho!" said Brer Terrapin to himself. "So they're after Brer Rabbit's sack of treasure, are they? I must tell him."

He crawled off to tell Brer Rabbit. "You'd better be sure to keep that door locked," said Brer Terrapin. "Brer Fox and Brer Wolf come along each night hoping to get your sack of treasure."

Brer Rabbit grinned. "Is that so? Well, all I've got in my sack is carrots. Ho, they think it's treasure, do they, and they're after it! Well,

what about playing a little trick on them, Brer Terrapin?"

Brer Rabbit thought a bit and then he went off to market. He bought a whole lot of sponges, dry and sandy. He stuffed them tightly into a stout sack, and tied up the neck.

"Now, on the first wet night I'll leave the shed door unlocked," he said.

"And Brer Fox and Brer Wolf can pick up that sack. It'll give them a surprise long before they get home!"

The next night was stormy. Great black clouds poured down torrents of rain. Brer Rabbit wondered if Brer Fox and Brer Wolf would be along.

They came, holding umbrellas above their heads. Perhaps Brer Rabbit had forgotten to lock the shed this black, stormy night!

"He has!" whispered Brer Fox. "The door is open. Come on Brer Wolf—we'll soon get that sack of treasure!"

They felt about and came to the big sack of sponges. "Here's the sack," said Brer Fox. "I'll take my turn at carrying it first. My, it's not very heavy! That's queer."

"Hurry!" said Brer Wolf, thinking he heard a sound outside. "Maybe the treasure is paper money."

They went out into the night. Brer Rabbit and Brer Terrapin, who had been hiding under a nearby bush, followed the pair softly.

The rain poured down. Brer Fox couldn't use his umbrella as he was carrying the sack. It was soon soaking wet.

Then suddenly a weird voice rang out through the darkness, and Brer Fox almost dropped the sack in fright. The voice chanted a peculiar song:

"May the treasure break your back,
May your bones all creak and crack,
May you sink beneath the sack . . .
Bring it b-a-a-a-ack! Bring it ba-a-a-ack!"

"What's that?" whispered Brer Fox.

"Pooh! Only Brer Rabbit trying to frighten us into taking back the sack," said Brer Wolf. "Don't you know his voice? We're not going to take a scrap of notice."

They went on. The sponges in the sack began to get wet. They swelled up. They became heavier. Brer Fox began to pant.

"What's the matter?" said Brer Wolf. "That sack isn't heavy!"

"It's almost breaking my back!" panted Brer Fox. "You take a turn. It was so light to begin with."

Brer Wolf took the sack. He was most astonished at the unexpected weight. "My, it's heavy!" he said, and staggered along beneath it.

"Are your bones creaking and cracking?" asked Brer Fox, anxiously. "Oh, my goodness, I hope Brer Rabbit hasn't put a spell on this sack! You heard what he said about our backs breaking, and our bones cracking."

"And he said we'd sink beneath the sack!" groaned Brer Wolf, staggering along. The rain had now soaked all the sponges through and through, and they were very, very heavy. They were bursting to get out of the sack. They became heavier.

Brer Wolf almost sank beneath the sack. He panted to Brer Fox in alarm. "We'd better take it back, Brer Fox. You know what tricks Brer Rabbit can play. Better take it back before we come to any harm."

Brer Fox was alarmed. He agreed with Brer Wolf and the two of them turned back. They went right back to Brer Rabbit's shed and staggered in with the sack of sponges.

A lantern flashed on them. Brer Rabbit was behind them at the door. "Oho!" he said, grinning. "So you've taken my sponges for a walk and brought them back again. How kind of you!"

The swollen sponges could no longer find room in the sack. They burst it—and in front of Brer Fox and Brer Wolf, who stared at them in amazement, dozens of soaked sponges rolled on to the floor!

"Sponges!" said Brer Fox, in a hollow voice.

"Sponges!" said Brer Wolf. "No wonder they felt so light when we set out—and got so heavy when the rain soaked them. Brer Rabbit, this is a trick!" Brer Wolf was very angry.

"Serves you right," said Brer Rabbit. "You meant to play a trick on me and take my sack of treasure, didn't you? Well, that's it over there, see! You can't complain if I play a trick on *you*. And don't look as if you're going to eat me. I've got Mr. Dog to supper tonight, and he'll be after you if I give so much as a squeak!"

And with that Brer Rabbit went out of the shed, whistling. Brer Fox nudged Brer Wolf. "What about the real sack of treasure? Come on!"

They hauled away the sack Brer Rabbit had pointed to—and, my, that was heavy all right. Then away they fled in the darkness.

Brer Terrapin and Brer Rabbit rolled about on the ground, laughing till they nearly killed themselves.

As for Brer Fox and Brer Wolf, they hurried home in delight. But when they opened that sack, what do you suppose they found inside it? Why, nothing but old rotten potatoes! Brer Rabbit had tricked them again!

And the next time Brer Rabbit met them he held his nose with his paw. "Pooh!" he said, "you smell of rotten potatoes! Don't you come near *me*, Brer Fox and Brer Wolf!"

Brer Rabbit's a Rascal

NOW, ONCE when Brer Rabbit was hard at work scraping the stones off his bit of ground, he heard a cry for help. Off he went, rake in hand, to see what the matter was.

It was the little girl belonging to the farmer. She had been fishing in the river and had slipped and fallen in. "Save me," she cried, and went swirling past Brer Rabbit, her skirt spreading out on the water.

Well, old Brer Rabbit he ran beside her, jabbing with his rake. And at last he got hold of the little girl's belt and hauled her to the bank. There she sat, sobbing and crying, her arms round Brer Rabbit's neck.

"You come home to your Ma," said Brer Rabbit. "You're wet. She'll dry you and give you a good hot drink."

So off they went together, the little girl clinging to Brer Rabbit as if she would never let him go. And my word, when the farmer heard how he had saved his little girl there wasn't anything he wouldn't have done for old good-hearted Brer Rabbit.

"There's a sack of carrots over there," he said. "Take it. And there's a sack of potatoes, too. You're welcome to it. And while you're about, help yourself to a sack of turnips. You're a born rascal, Brer Rabbit, but you're good-hearted, so you are! Now off you go while I still think good of you!"

Now, when Brer Rabbit was wheeling home his three sacks, whistling a merry song and feeling on top of the world, who should come along but

Brer Fox, Brer Bear and Brer Wolf. How they stared when they saw Brer Rabbit with so much food!

"Carrots! Turnips! Potatoes! Sacks of them!" said Brer Fox. "Hey, Brer Rabbit, give us some. And don't tell us you've come by them honestly, because we shan't believe you!"

Brer Rabbit was most annoyed. "You go and ask the farmer!" he said. "He gave me them with kind words, so he did!"

"Now you're telling stories," said Brer Wolf. "You give us some of those carrots and turnips and potatoes Brer Rabbit or we'll come along one night and help ourselves!"

"I *might* have given you some," said Brer Rabbit, wheeling his barrow away with his head in the air. "I *might* have given you some if you knew how to behave!"

Brer Bear, Brer Fox and Brer Wolf stared after Brer Rabbit. Brer Fox scratched his head. "Well, however he got those sacks he's going to share them with us, whether he wants to or not! Shall we go along to his place tonight and see where he's put the sacks?"

"Yes," said the other two, and Brer Fox grinned at them. "Meet me here. We'll slip along in the shadows—and my, won't Brer Rabbit be angry in the morning!"

Now, old Brer Rabbit had a kind of feeling that Brer Fox, Brer Wolf and Brer Bear might be along that night. He wheeled his sacks to his shed and emptied all the carrots, potatoes and turnips out on the ground. He picked out the bad ones and set them aside. Then he took a big broom and swept all the roots along the ground to his cellar.

Bumpity-bumpity-bump—they rolled down into his cellar and he shut and locked the door. Then he went back to the shed again. He took the sacks to the pile of stones he had scraped off his ground and he filled them almost to the top with the stones. But right at the very top he didn't put the stones—he put a layer of bad carrots, a layer of poor potatoes, and in the third sack a layer of rotten turnips. Oh, Brer Rabbit, you're a wily one!

He dragged the sacks back to his shed and set them up against the walls. Then he went indoors, leaving the shed door unlocked.

"And if this isn't a nice easy way of getting rid of all those stones, well, I'll never know a better one!" said old Brer Rabbit.

Now, that night along crept Brer Fox, Brer Bear and Brer Wolf. There was a little moon so they kept well in the shadows. They came to the shed and tried the door. It wasn't locked—that was fine!

They slipped inside. Brer Bear pointed to the three sacks in glee. He looked in the top of one. He could see dimly in the moonlight—and he saw a layer of potatoes!

"Here are the potatoes," he said. "I'll take this sack. You follow with the others, Brer Wolf and Brer Fox."

They staggered out with the sacks. "My sack is mighty heavy!" said Brer Fox. "I never thought turnips could be such a dreadful weight."

"These carrots are heavy, too," panted Brer Wolf. "My, they must be good solid ones!"

Brer Rabbit saw the three of them through his window, staggering up

18

the lane in the shadows. He grinned to himself. "Nice of them to carry those tiresome stones!" he said. "I must thank them when I see them!"

Well, by the time Brer Fox, Brer Wolf and Brer Bear had reached their homes they couldn't walk a step farther! They sank down on the ground, panting. Brer Bear thought he would make some potato soup and he shook the sack hard—and out came six potatoes—and about twenty stones!

Then Brer Bear knew he had been tricked and he rushed to tell Brer Fox and Brer Wolf. But they had already found out, and dear me, the names they called old Brer Rabbit would have made his whiskers curl if he had heard them!

Brer Rabbit went out of his way to meet the three the next day. He raised his hat politely and gave his very best bow.

"My best thanks, gentlemen, for so kindly removing all those stones for me," he said. "I shall have another sackful tomorrow if one of you would like to call for it."

And then, my goodness me, he had to run for his life—but he didn't mind that because Brer Rabbit could always run faster than anyone else. As for Brer Bear, Brer Wolf and Brer Fox, they had to carry all the stones out of their gardens and empty them into the ditch. They were so stiff afterwards that they couldn't walk properly for days!

Ah, Brer Rabbit, it's hard to get the better of you, you rascal!

When Brer Rabbit Melted

"I'T's hot!" said Brer Rabbit, panting, as he scampered through the wood. "Hotter than ever! I shall melt, I know I shall!"

He sat down under a big tree and fanned himself with a leaf. He puffed and he panted. He wished he could take off his warm fur coat, but he couldn't. He wished he could unbutton his ears and lay them aside, but he couldn't do that either.

"I must just go on being hot. But I shall melt," said Brer Rabbit. "I know I shall!"

"Then I'll come along and lick you up!" said a voice, and to Brer Rabbit's horror he saw Brer Fox peering round a tree at him. Brer Rabbit leapt to his feet at once.

He scurried off—but round another tree came Brer Bear, fat and heavy. He made a grab with his big paw at Brer Rabbit and knocked him flat. Before poor Brer Rabbit could get up, Brer Fox pounced on him and held him tight.

"Got you at last, Brer Rabbit!" said Brer Fox. "And I'll take you home with me and have you for supper tonight."

"Wait a bit!" said Brer Bear. "I was the one that knocked him down! I'll take him home to my wife for *my* supper!"

"Well, you won't," said Brer Fox. "I've been after Brer Rabbit for a very long time. If anyone is going to eat him, *I* am!"

"Now, you look here, Brer Fox," began Brer Bear, "you let me have my say. I'm going to eat Brer Rabbit, not you. My wife could do with a rabbit-pie. If anyone is going to eat him, *I* am!"

"Wouldn't she rather have a pot of new honey?" asked Brer Fox.

Brer Bear looked doubtful. He and his wife liked honey better than anything. But was this a little trick of Brer Fox's? He wasn't sure.

"I'll come home with you and help you to drag Brer Rabbit along," he said. "Then, if you show me the honey, I might say 'yes'."

"You let me go!" said Brer Rabbit, who was still underneath the paws of both Brer Bear and Brer Fox, and didn't like it a bit.

When they got to Brer Fox's house, they tied Brer Rabbit to a chair so that he couldn't move. Then Brer Fox and Brer Bear began to argue.

"You take my pot of honey and leave me Brer Rabbit," said Brer Fox, who didn't think there would be much pie left for him if Brer Bear shared his supper.

"Well, I don't think I will, till I know if Mrs. Bear wants me to," said Brer Bear, being very annoying.

"Well, go and ask her," said Brer Fox.

"Certainly not," said Brer Bear. "You'd eat Brer Rabbit up as soon as my back was turned! *You* go and ask her."

"Ho! And have you gobble up Brer Rabbit as soon as I was out of the house!" said Brer Fox. "No, thank you!"

"You let me go!" wailed Brer Rabbit, wriggling in the ropes that bound him to a chair.

The others took no notice of him. They glared angrily at one another. "Well, we'll leave Brer Rabbit tied up in this chair, and we'll lock the door, and I'll go to Mrs. Bear, whilst you sit *outside* the locked door," said Brer Fox, at last. "See, Brer Bear? I shall take the key in my pocket, so that you can't go in and eat up Brer Rabbit. He can't escape because he's all tied up. I'll be back as soon as I can to tell you what Mrs. Bear says."

As soon as Brer Rabbit was left alone he began to wriggle like mad. He managed to get his mouth down to one of the ropes, and he began to gnaw and gnaw.

Soon he gnawed right through the rope. It didn't take him long to get free then! He skipped to the windows. Alas, they were too heavy for him to open. He tried and he tried, but it was no good.

"*Now* what shall I do?" thought Brer Rabbit. "I haven't much time, Brer Fox will soon be back."

Then he grinned all over his whiskery face. He went back to his chair and tied up the ropes again. Then he hunted about for a soft broom, and pulled out a handful of hairs, which were very like his own whiskers. He scattered them on the chair seat.

He found some cotton wool, and put a round dob of it on the chair seat, too. It looked exactly like his white bobtail.

Then he noticed some roses in a bowl. He took them out and broke off their big, curved thorns. He put some of the thorns on the chair seat and some on the floor. They looked like claws!

He chuckled to himself and put the roses back into the bowl, without

thorns. Then he began to wail and howl.

"Oh, I'm so hot! Brer Bear, let me free. I tell you I'm melting!"

"You can't trick me like that, Brer Rabbit," said Brer Bear. "You're not melting! You just want to make me open this door and you'll jump out. But I shan't. Anyway, old Brer Fox has got the key."

Brer Rabbit went on howling. "I'm melting. Oh, my legs have melted! Oh, now my tail's melting! And there goes my body! I'll soon be melted completely if nobody helps me!"

Now, as soon as he heard Brer Fox coming back, Brer Rabbit shot into the coal-scuttle that stood near the door, pulled some bits of coal over himself, and lay quite still. He heard Brer Fox unlocking the door and talking to Brer Bear.

"Mrs. Bear says she'd rather have the honey. I'll get it and you can take it to her and leave Brer Rabbit with me."

"He's been howling and moaning all the time that he's melting with the heat," said Brer Bear. The door opened and the two walked in. They stopped at once when they saw the loose ropes and the empty chair.

"Where's he gone?" yelled Brer Fox, and darted to the door in case Brer Rabbit should appear from some hiding place and run out.

Brer Bear stared in alarm at the empty chair. He saw the long hairs there, like whiskers; he saw the white patch of wool, like a bobtail; and he saw the rose-thorns that looked exactly like claws.

"Brer Fox! He's melted! He said he was, and he has! Look—there's only his tail, his whiskers and his claws left! I tell you, Brer Fox, it's the end of him—poor old Brer Rabbit has melted!"

Brer Fox came to see. He stared in amazement at the whiskers, the bobtail and claws. How could Brer Rabbit have melted like that? But it certainly looked as if he had!

"Yes, he's gone," said Brer Fox. "No rabbit-pie tonight. Well, good riddance to him. He was always tricking me, that rabbit. He won't trick me any more."

From the front gate came a cheeky voice: "Heyo, Brer Fox! Heyo Brer Bear! Isn't it hot? I do declare it's so hot that I'm melting!"

And there was that rascal of a Brer Rabbit laughing fit to kill himself. He had tricked old Brer Fox properly—and it wouldn't be long before he did it again—and again—*and* again!